P9-CSH-296

PAPA tells CHITA a STORY

by Elizabeth Fitzgerald Howard
illustrated by Floyd Cooper

Simon & Schuster Books for Young Readers

To all our family's storytellers and griots—
with special thanks to Chita and Uncle Harry

—E. F. H.

For Virginia Duncan

—F. C.

SIMON & SCHUSTER BOOKS FOR YOUNG READERS
An imprint of Simon & Schuster Children's Publishing Division
1230 Avenue of the Americas
New York, NY 10020
Text copyright © 1995 by Elizabeth Fitzgerald Howard
Illustrations copyright © 1995 by Floyd Cooper
SIMON & SCHUSTER BOOKS FOR YOUNG READERS is a trademark of Simon & Schuster.
Designed by Christy Hale
The text of this book is set in Tiffany Medium.
The illustrations are rendered in oil wash on board and mixed media.
Manufactured in Hong Kong by South China Printing Company (1988) Ltd.
10   9   8   7   6   5   4   3   2   1
Library of Congress Cataloging-in-Publication Data
Howard, Elizabeth Fitzgerald.
Papa tells Chita a story / by Elizabeth Fitzgerald Howard ;
illustrated by Floyd Cooper.—1st ed.
p.   cm.
Summary: A young African-American girl shares a special time with
her father as he tells her about when he was a soldier in Cuba
during the Spanish-American War.
ISBN 0-02-744623-9
1. Spanish-American War, 1898—Juvenile fiction.   [1. Spanish-
American War, 1898—Fiction.   2. Fathers and daughters—Fiction.
3. Afro-Americans—Fiction.]   I. Cooper, Floyd, ill.   II. Title.
PZ7.H83273Pap   1995
[E]—dc20   93-1252

A NOTE FROM THE AUTHOR

The Spanish-American War (1898) erupted when the United States decided to help Cuba free itself from Spanish control. African-American regiments participated—the 24th and 25th infantries, and the 9th and 10th calvaries—and eventually several state national guard units accepted black volunteers. The newly free black citizens welcomed the opportunity to serve outside of the United States, and black newspapers reported the widely held view that this would be a way for blacks to prove their worth. Black soldiers fought alongside Theodore Roosevelt's Rough Riders in the charge up San Juan Hill and at Santiago. They were commended in a note in the *Review of Reviews* (October 1898): "The Negro soldiers showed excellent discipline, the highest qualities of personal bravery, very superior physical endurance, unfailing good temper, and the most generous disposition toward all comrades in arms, whether white or black." But letters to black papers from Negro soldiers reflected their anger at the constant harassment and humiliation due to prevailing attitudes and prejudicial army regulations. Fighting for their country did not lead to glory.

My cousin Chita's father, Harry S. McCard, enlisted in order to earn experience and money for his intended medical education. He might have been involved, as were some of the black recruits, in helping to care for victims of yellow fever, a foe fiercer than Spain. McCard's actual role is no longer known, but he did display a medal. "Perhaps it was for good conduct," Chita says.

Chita remembers how her father often told her an exciting story about a brave and scary mission on which he carried an important message to the other side of Cuba. Swamps, alligators, and eagles all had to be overcome. It was awesome! But one day Papa told the story differently, reversing some of the incidents, and Chita protested, "Papa, you didn't tell it that way last time." Chita says Papa never told the story again.

In the tradition of the tall tale, I have extended and exaggerated Chita's recollection of Papa's story.

—E.F.H.

The passage from *Review of Reviews* is quoted in "Spanish-American War: Negro Participation (1898)" in *Afro-American Encyclopedia* (North Miami, FL: Educational Book Publishers, 1974), 2550. See also "Black Servicemen and the Military Establishment: The Spanish-American War (1898)" in *The Negro Almanac: A Reference Work on the African American* 5th ed., Harry A. Ploski and James Williams eds. and comps. (Detroit, MI: Gale, 1989), 842-844. Letters from African-American soldiers, written primarily to the black newspapers, have been collected in *"Smoked Yankees" and the Struggle for Empire: Letters from Negro Soldiers, 1898–1902*, by William B. Gatewood, Jr. (Urbana, IL: University of Illinois Press, 1971).

෧ PAPA TIME, CHITA TIME

After supper is Papa time for Chita.
"Hurry, hurry, Mama," says Chita.
Chita is helping Mama with the supper dishes.
She can dry the spoons and forks very quickly,
whisk, whisk.
But she must dry the china plates and cups slowly
and very carefully.

Papa is sitting in his big chair by the fireplace. He
has had a busy day helping sick patients. Some came
to his office at home, just next to the living room.
Some he went out to see in their own houses. Papa
rode to his house calls in the big buggy pulled along
by Henry the horse.

But now Papa is resting and reading and waiting for
Chita.
After supper is Chita time for Papa.

๑ *A STORY, A STORY*

"Papa, I'm ready!"
Chita pulls her own small chair close to Papa's big one.

"A story, a story. What story shall we have tonight?" Papa asks.

"Papa, Papa," pleads Chita, "tell about how you were the bravest soldier and carried the message and won the war!"

Papa smiles.
"All right, my muchachita, I will tell you about those exciting days. And you can help me tell this story!"

⊚ *BRAVE PAPA*

"Once, when I was a young man, I decided to become a doctor. I had to earn some money to go to medical school, so I joined the army and went off to fight in the Spanish War.

"I had just arrived in Cuba when the colonel called us all together.

" 'Men,' he said, 'we don't have enough soldiers to capture this hill. And we must have more supplies. I need someone very brave to carry a secret message to our troops across the island. It is a long and dangerous trip. There are snakes and swamps . . .' "

"And alligators, Papa," whispers Chita with a shivery giggle.

"That's right, Chita, and a high hill covered with brambles and prickles. Then the colonel asked, 'Who will go? Who is my bravest soldier?' "

"And it was you, Papa! You said, 'I will go!' " shouts Chita.

"Well . . . I wanted to be brave," says Papa. "So I said, 'I will do it, sir.' The colonel gave me an oilskin pouch with a letter inside. And a canteen full of water. And a map. And Majestic, a dark sleek horse with a waving white tail.

"I left immediately, riding Majestic. It was fiercely hot in the tropical sun. We rode through wide fields of tall tall grass. Suddenly Majestic stopped. Something was slithering and sneaking in the tall tall grass. *Sswushush . . . sswushush . . .* What could it be?"

"It was the big big BIG snake, Papa!"

"You're right, Chita! The snake was brown and round and as long as this living room. It raised up its head, squinted its beady eyes, and squinched toward us. But Majestic reared his front legs and zigzagged through the field, while I waved my sword and shouted strong words. We confused that snake, and it snake-snaked away in another direction."

"Hurray for Majestic! Hurray for Papa!" cries Chita. "And you kept on riding!"

"Well, I kept on riding, riding, riding . . . and the sun got hotter, hotter, hotter. And after a while we came to a great gray-green, greasy and slimy . . . "

"Swamp, Papa! It was the swamp!"

"Ugh! Chita! Ugh! I had to get through the swamp to reach the other side of the island. But Majestic would not move forward. I tried to persuade him. But he just stood there, still as a stone. I was disgusted. So I climbed down and told him, 'Good-bye. Go home, horse,' and he turned and headed back toward the colonel's camp. Then I stepped into the wet ooze. I held the colonel's oilskin pouch tight. Ooh, it was dreadful. I got in deeper and deeper. And just as I was about halfway across . . ."

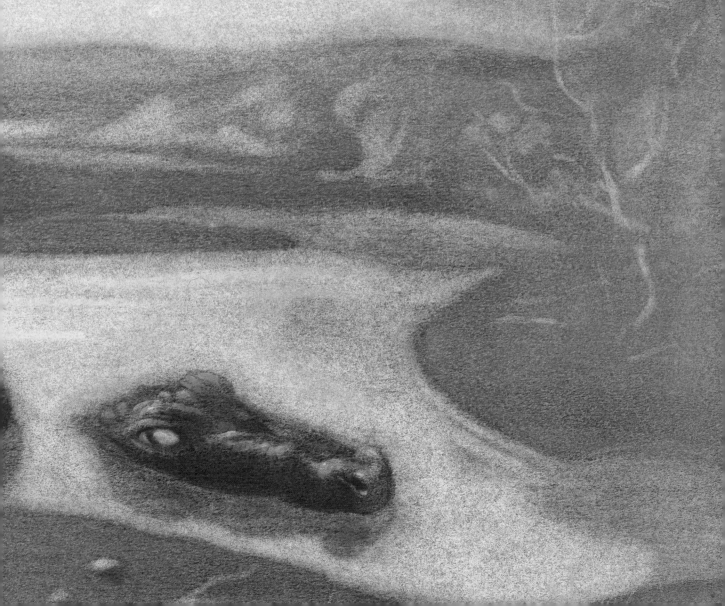

"The alligator, Papa!"

"Yes, indeedy, Chita! That alligator eyed me and came
swimming steadily toward me. He yawned open his
wide mouth, and I could count his sharp teeth.
What could I do? I stuck the oilskin pouch deep into
my shirt and hoped the message would be safe. Then
I took a big breath, ducked under, and started
swimming. Hard work in the mucky slime, with that
alligator thrashing about above me!
Gluoosh . . . glush . . . gluoosh!"

"And you swam right under the alligator, Papa, didn't you?" giggles Chita.
"Just swam right under him! Ha!
I tricked the old rascal! He couldn't catch me!
At last I climbed out onto dry land.
I had lost my sword, and lost my gun, and lost my canteen . . . but . . ."

"But the oilskin pouch was safe, Papa!"

"Yes, Chita. And, ooch, I was so sticky and muddy . . .
but luckily I came to a waterfall. I stood under the
cool cool tumbling water and washed off all the slimy
ooze. But by now it was getting dark."

"And you were a teeny teeny bit scared, Papa!"

"A teeny teeny bit, Chita! And wet. And tired. But in front of me was a high hill."

"Very very high," says Chita. "And covered with brambles and prickles!"

"And I wondered if I could climb through all that thick underbrush. But I had to do it. I climbed and I crawled. And I crawled and I climbed. The brambles and prickles scratched my arms and legs. By the light of the moon I kept crawling and climbing, and at last—about midnight—I got to the top!"

"And you saw the big bird's nest, Papa!"

"Oh yes, Chita. In the moonlight I saw what looked like a big bird's nest! And it was empty! I was so weary and worn that I took a chance. I climbed in, curled up, and fell asleep."

"And then you heard the very very scary noise, Papa!" Chita whispers.

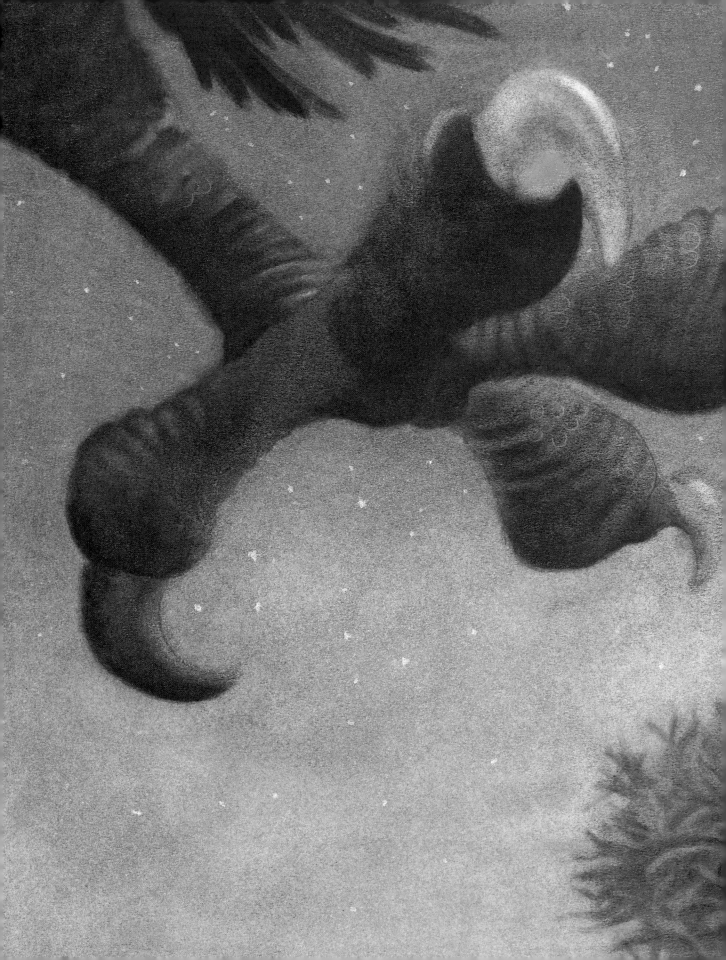

"You're right, Chita! I woke up to a loud screeching sound. *Skreeeeeech!* Help! I nearly jumped out of my skin! A giant eagle was scolding because somebody was in her nest!"

"Papa, *you* were in her nest!"

"She flew toward me with her claws outstretched. *Skreech! Skreeeeeech!* I was terrified. I scrambled out and started stumbling my way down the other side of the hill. It was rough and tough, and I was scratched and sore. . . . After a long time, when I was almost at the bottom . . ."

"It was getting light! And you could smell something, Papa!" cheers Chita.

"What was it, Chita?"

"You're right, Chita!" says Papa. "I went up to the officer in charge. 'Sir,' I said, 'I am Private McCard. I have brought an urgent message from the colonel.' And I handed him the oilskin pouch. 'Thank you,' said the officer. He took out the letter and read the message. Then he looked at me. 'McCard, you are extraordinarily brave. I will send more soldiers to the colonel immediately.' "

"And he sent more soldiers. And you went with them. And everybody was brave. But I think you were the bravest, Papa!"

⊚ WHAT IS TRUE?

Chita jumps up and hugs Papa. Then she takes an old hat down from a peg on the wall and puts it on her head. And she takes a worn-looking belt from the bookcase and buckles it around her waist. "Here is your hat from the war, Papa! And here is your belt."

And then, proudly, she pulls open a small drawer in Papa's big desk.

"And here is your beautiful medal!" Chita beams. She holds up a bronze medal with a red, white, and blue ribbon tied through it and hands it to Papa.

"You're right, Chita," Papa replies with a smile and a faraway look in his eyes. He turns the medal around and around in his hands.

"Papa, is that a true story?" Chita asks. Chita always likes to ask Papa if something is true.

"Well, my little muchachita," says Papa. "Some is true, and some is not true. But this is my true soldier's hat, and this is my true soldier's belt. And this is my true medal for being a brave soldier in the Spanish War. All that is true." Papa tweaks Chita's nose. "But do you know what else is true?"

"What, Papa!"

"It's true that you are a very good girl, and that Mama is waiting for you! Because it's time to go to bed!"

"Papa, you're a funny man," Chita says as she squeezes him a good-night hug.

"Good night, Papa!"

"Good night, Chita!"